Vampire Apocalypse

Know Your Enemy

A Survival Guide

By Rex Cutty

Foreword

Look, I'm not going to tell you who I am, so quit asking. You just freaking don't need to know because you're either going to believe what I have to say about dealing with the undead or you're not. Same deal as when we were talking about zombies. People who want to live don't need to check my résumé. Which is good, since I don't have one.

But okay, fine. I'll tell you the basics again. I'm not ex-black ops. Not SEAL trained, although those guys are seriously bad ass. I'm not SWAT. Biggest thing I've got going for me? I'm alive. I intend to stay that way.

I don't intend to sit around waiting on some expert to teach me anything about how to accomplish that goal because, hello? Twenty-first century? Internet? If you read it you will learn?

Get onboard and take some personal responsibility for God's sake. Which I'm gonna assume you're prepared to do since you're bothering to read this book. First thing you need to deal with? The vampires are already here. They've been here for centuries.

Vampires invented the science of flying under the radar. — No, moron, they don't actually fly and they don't turn into bats. Really? — Vampire are good at not being *noticed*, not standing out. Why? Because it's seriously in their best interests to integrate themselves into our society.

If there is one thing those bloodsuckers know it's how to

play power games and come out on top. A vampire is born to be a politician. In fact, many of them are politicians.

You can engage in all the elegant medical theorizing you want to and you can be one of those bleeding hearts and talk about curing the vampires, but it's not going to get you anywhere but bleeding yourself.

Vampires aren't like us. In fact, I think they're a completely different species, so how are you going to cure something from being what nature designed it to be?

When you're talking survival, you have to be prepared for all the different kinds of excrement that might hit the rotary device.

My granddaddy had himself a bomb shelter back during the Cold War. Nobody pulled the trigger on the missiles, but if they had, Gramps would have made it.

So what do we have to worry about these days? Oh hell, I don't know.

- **Pandemics from viruses like H1N1.** That's bird flu in case you don't know it. Think the flu is no big deal? Between 1918 and 1919 the Spanish flu wiped out 20-50 million worldwide and infected 500 million.

- **Climate change.** Think the bleeding hearts just made that one up? Guess what. Global warming is happening faster than any other change the planet's seen in 65 million years. By the end of the century annual temperatures could spike by a little better than 40 degrees.

Then there's lovely little contenders like an asteroid slamming into us, some massive volcano going off, one of our happily little genetically modified organisms running amuck, or global system collapse from a ripple economic / political crisis — or maybe we actually build SkyNet and artificial intelligence proves humans really are obsolete meat sacks.

Cheerful stuff, huh? Those are just the ones the scientists are willing to admit they're worried about. Uh huh. The CDC zombie pandemic plan is just a joke. Right. Absolutely. And Nixon didn't have a paranoid bone in his body.

Let me tell you something, pal. Zombies are a piece of cake compared to vampires. Zombies don't think. Yeah, they can come at you with a really dangerous herd mentality, but they're just reacting to sound and probably scent.

Vampires have steel trap minds. They see everything. They hear everything. They remember everything. They have the patience to wait out trends and developments that best serve their interests.

I mean honestly, when you're pretty much immortal — as long as you avoid sunlight and a stake to the heart — you can afford to be patient.

You put their patience up against our impatience, and brother, we could well be screwed. We are really, really good at messing up the planet we're living on.

We're also really, really good at sending society straight to hell in a hand basket. Humans are perfectly capable of being fat, lazy, corrupt, clueless dumb asses.

When we act like that, which is entirely too often, we create gaps and holes vampires can and do exploit to leverage themselves into a position of power.

- I can teach you how to spot a vampire.

- I can teach you how to protect yourself in his presence and even to take him out.

- I can't re-educate a whole society that is so damned out of touch with reality it leaves the biggest backdoor of them all open — political power.

Last election, about 57.5 % of all eligible voters bothered to go to the polls and that's just because one of the guys running was, how shall we say it, problematic for a large portion of the electorate.

In the end, the thing that will send the human race the way of the dinosaurs is our lethargy. Sometimes we make garden slugs look energetic and purposeful.

You don't think so? Then tell me why in the hell we have a U.S. Congress with the lowest approval rating in this country's history and we just keep re-electing the same fricking saps?

It's not all that hard to stay alive in any kind of apocalypse in a practical sense. I've said it before and I'll say it again, the Rule of Three applies:

- Three minutes without oxygen.
- Three hours without shelter in climate extremes.
- Three days without water.
- Three weeks without food.

You get on top of those things and stay away from the morons, you'll make it. But negotiate the halls of power with creatures several centuries old that cut their fangs on the politics of the Roman Empire?

It's like I'm trying to tell you saps, vampires aren't like the other things that go bump in the night. They're in a league all their own, and most of us aren't anywhere up to playing in the majors with them.

Acknowledgments

Acknowledge this… to all bloodsuckers trust when I say that you will regret crossing my path!

Yours Truly,

Rex

Table of Contents

Table of Contents

Chapter 1 - What Are We Dealing With?

So, you got your garlic and a cross. Fantastic. Let me know how the lasagna and your last communion turns out, because if that's all you've got against a vampire? Baby, you might as well open a vein and save the sucker the trouble.

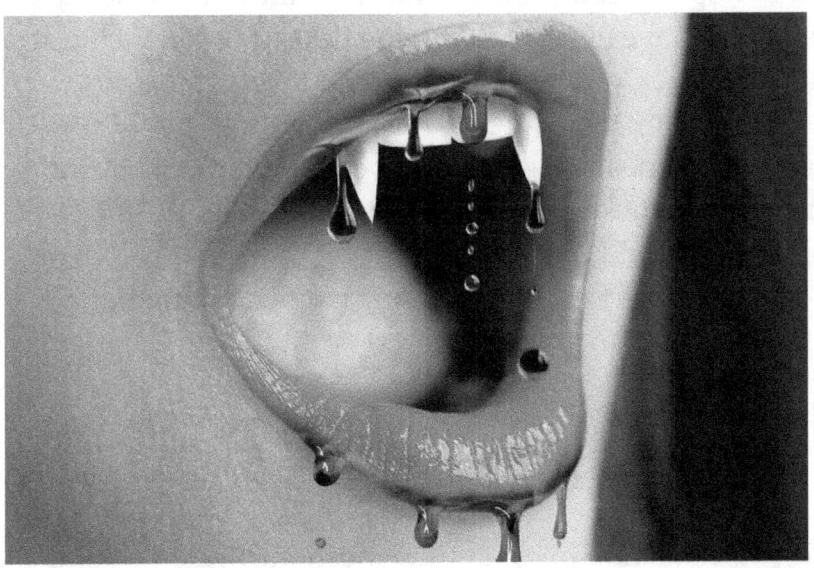

Didn't your Mama ever tell you what happens to girls who are easy? Maybe she didn't factor the undead into her personal bad boy equation, but you better do the math for yourself.

Rule #1 - Vampire groupies are the first ones stepping up to be on the menu. You pet rattlesnakes, too?

Don't get all smug and superior guys. Sell it to somebody who's buying. A vamp chick in black leather hits you up and you'll be donating your O-positive before the alley door slams. Believe you me, before she's done, she'll make that twisted sap from Fifty Shades of Whatever look like a choirboy.

When the Lady is a Vamp she's definitely too hungry to wait for dinner at eight. Have eight for dinner? Different matter. Blood's pretty low cal. It's one "lifestyle" where a woman can have everything on the dessert menu including you, baby cakes, and never gain an ounce.

In fact, that's one of the major attractions for the vampire groupies. Get sucked into this club, pun intended, and you'll never need Botox again. You get immortality (barring one of several ways a vampire can be killed) along with good looks that never fade.

This is not a cool lifestyle, people. Dead's dead, even when you accessorize the hell out of the condition.

So, if you can climb up out of the mosh pit while you still have a functioning brain cell, let's get serious here. We're bothering to talk about vampires at all because you people are not getting a pretty simple message.

Playing with monsters is a *bad* idea.

Last time I tried to get between you saps and disaster we were talking zombies. Let me try to explain how the supernatural social register works, because we've climbed up several rungs when the topic is vampires.

The Supernatural Social Register

Zombies, the current rage with the general public, are basically the white trash of the undead world. Totally low class, indiscriminate bottom feeders.

When you got a dead man walking because he's a zombie, doesn't matter who he was when he was alive. Once he bites the dust, he's as déclassé as the stiff shambling to his left.

Now, vampires? They've got some serious class and a level of political sophistication that makes the crowd in Washington, D.C. look like a bunch of rank posers. Vampires prefer to move in aristocratic circles. They may slum long enough for a quick snack on some junk food, but that's not where they spend their time and real efforts. They're invariably wealthy and well connected.

It takes a lot more work and resources to stay alive once you're dead. Vamps have serious mojo, they maintain a completely hidden society working in the shadows of the one we're running.

They have a culture built around keeping them alive, maintaining their preferred lifestyle, and building their power base.

How did they get their wealth and influence? They accumulated it over centuries. Let's just play with the numbers for a minute.

If you save $2,096.61 cents per month for 30 years, you'll have a million dollars. You follow that strategy for 500 years you'll wind up with $16.6 million. Now, that's not factoring in some pretty major financial options and factors:

- investments
- interest rates
- take overs
- coups
- blackmail
- extortion
- mergers
- acquisitions
- inflation
- deflation
- rates of exchange
- out and out theft

Vampires don't work for a living, but they love to broker power. A couple of grand a month is chump change for even the lowest level vamp.

Depending on when he was made, he could have priceless works of art in his collection, timed to sell at just the right moment. Need a little more investment capital? Turn a multi-millionaire and amass his fortune and connections.

This isn't just a single line of power we're talking about, it's a *web* that builds and expands over centuries. It's constructed on intricate alliances, agreements, old notes that come due, grudges, and feuds.

Some guy who was turned in the Seventies and is still dressing like an extra for *Saturday Night Fever* is not nearly as scary as a guy who was turned in the 1670s and has had almost 350 years to get his moves down. But once Dead Disco Guy starts getting connected in the broader web of vampire society, his level of scary moves up exponentially.

Vampires are not just living in our world, buddy, they're *influencing* it, which is what makes surviving a potential vampire "apocalypse" a whole lot more complicated than getting out of the way of a zombie.

When you get right down to it, zombies are just like cockroaches. Don't let one live or he'll come back with 500 of his closest friends and relatives.

But *one* well-placed vampire is all you need to have a world of trouble on your hands.

Vampires are all about *integration*. If the vamps leverage themselves into a position of power, it's not going to be some sloppy hamburger fest like the Z-men would pull off. The vamps will take over legally and make us think it's a good idea in the process.

Vamps are elegant, refined, charming, and damned efficient. You're dealing with a different class of monster here, brother, so be prepared to up your game -- and I don't mean by renting every vampire movie you can get your hands on.

Pop culture references won't save your jugular when the

fangs come out, and there's a reason for that. The vamps are using pop culture to fuel a classic campaign of disinformation.

Pop Culture Is a Vampire Tool

I don't know how I can be any clearer about this. Vampires are using pop culture against us. They want us buying a load of crap about their heritage, society, and plans.

Vampires want us to think it's cool to dress like loser goths, hang out in blood bars, and go all Renfield in our adoration of their immortal greatness.

They want us to want them and from where I'm sitting, it's working. In fact, the shrinks even have a name for that kind of vampire wanna-be delusion, "clinical vampirism."

Clinical Vampirism

Yep, it's a diagnosis, but I bet you'll have a hard time getting your insurance company to pay for it. The shrinks call it Renfield's Syndrome. The symptoms include:

- vampiric fantasies
- drinking blood (someone else's or your own)
- necrophilia (getting off on dead bodies)
- necrophagia (chowing down on dead bodies)
- cannibalism
- sadism

They were a little late to the party, but two eggheads put this one in the "psychiatric literature" in 1964 based on their analysis of two cases.

Now, the condition isn't found in the Diagnostic and Statistical Manual of Mental Disorders or the International Classification of Disease, but the doctors still peg it for a known if "uncommon psychiatric syndrome."

Let's just think about the original Renfield here for a minute. He was an inmate in a nut house who spent his days eating bugs because Dracula was controlling his every freaking thought. Sign me up — not!

There's no pop culture glamour involved in being anyone's "servant." I'll take my chances with the zombies before I become some vampire's errand boy. So why do so many people do it? Oldest motivation in the world, sex.

Fifty Shades of Vampire

In this department, Uncle Rex cannot offer you any personal insights. I like my women with a pulse. But apparently, sex with a vampire is supposed to be fantastic.

First off, a lot of vamps really don't go for the neck, which immediately turns some groupies on. A vampire's idea of safe sex is to opt for a bigger straw in a more private area -- the femoral artery in the groin.

Besides better blood flow while they're feeding, the bite can't be seen when the donor is dressed. Much better to keep everything on the down low. And yeah, lots of vamps swing in both directions.

Remember, hitting the sack is not about the sex for them, moron, it's about the blood. As long as it tastes good, the shape of the bottle doesn't matter.

And the fastest way to get you to offer up their next meal is to get you thinking with body parts that do *not* involve your brain.

We'll talk more about the fact that vamps can control the effect of their bites, but add to the list the fact that they can make you see fireworks in the bedroom at just the moment they sink their fangs into your body. But you pay the price for all that great sex.

Look, I'm sorry to be direct — not. As far as I'm concerned opening your veins or arteries for a vamp just makes you another kind of junkie hooker. Crack is crack. One drug goes in, another one gets sucked out, but you're still just chasing a cheap high or turning a trick. Both can get you dead.

Does Blood Type Matter?

According to the Sookie Stackhouse, *True Blood*, vampire "unverse," blood type does matter. In that fictional take on the world of vamps, the bloodsuckers are out of the closet and they have synthetic, bottled blood at their disposal — offered up by type and best served just a little bit above room temperature.

In the real world when a vampire needs to eat, he's not particular about any of his victim's qualities, but if he's feeding regularly? Well, it's just as easy to bite a pretty woman or a handsome man as an ugly one.

So yeah, vampires have a physical type and they may think some blood tastes better than others. But from what I can tell, those preferences aren't so much a matter of blood type as "soul" type.

Just like everything else they "study," the scientists have done their best to make hematology all nice and clean and "factual," but metaphysically, there's nothing more alive and juiced up with energy and emotion than blood.

If that weren't the truth, wouldn't we talk about "bad" blood between families, and Foreigner couldn't have had a hit with *Hot Blooded*. Yeah, so sue me, I was alive in the Seventies. At least it wasn't the 1870s.

Most vamps will tell you blood tastes different based on the emotional state of the donor aka "the victim." This shouldn't come as a newsflash, but a lot of vampires will tell you the name of their favorite flavor, fear.

The Real Goal? Control the Next Generation

Right now there's all kind of "young adult" fiction out there making vampires look sensitive, misunderstood, and sexy as hell. Uh. Yeah. People. Ever hear of the Hitler Youth?

Here's a little *Mein Kampf* quote for you, "The state must declare the child to be the most precious treasure of the people. As long as the government is perceived as working for the benefit of the children, the people will happily endure almost any curtailment of liberty and almost any deprivation."

Repeat after me. "Curtailment. Of. Liberty."

Get the young people onboard and taking the whole society over is a piece of cake. I shouldn't have to point this out, unless you're six days older than dirt, but run this equation.

- young people + raging hormones x charismatic "leader" = (blood cult + blind loyalty)^2

Beyond all that. Young adult fiction? If that crap isn't evil, I don't know what is. Pablum and propaganda. Period.

Mainstreaming Vampires = BAD

Okay, so, back on this whole "mainstreaming" thing. This is where we start getting into trouble, people. Not to be all metaphysical-politically-repressive Joe McCarthy here or anything, but vampires campaigning for their civil rights is a hell of a lot scarier in my book than creeping socialism.

That whole multi-monster vibe the studio execs out in Hollywood got started in the 1940s is now so standard, we've got a whole lot of TV shows that have done the same thing. On the one hand, I get the symbolism. Yes, Rex is aware of nuances people.

Use all these creatures most people don't think exist and throw them into social situations and you've got some symbolism to put in front of the bigots. I get the message and it's a good one — race, color, gender, creed, and who you're doing don't say a damn thing about who you are. The shows are cool.

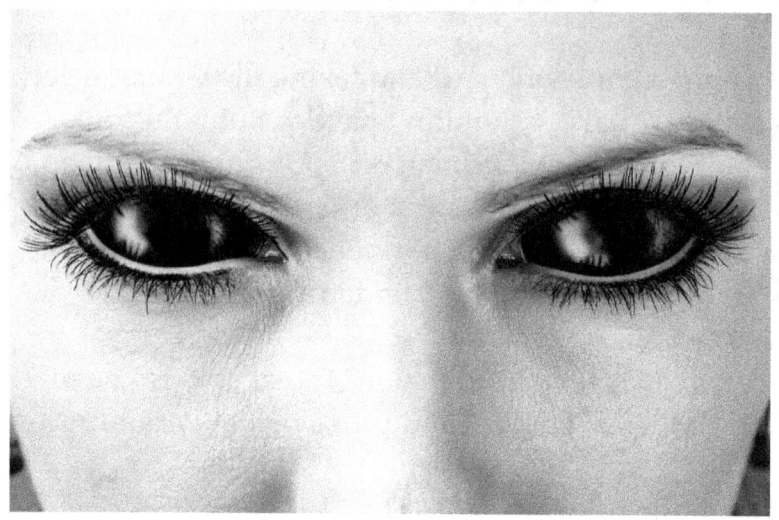

A smooth-talking, torch-singing, green-skinned demon ran a karaoke bar on *Buffy*. Who's not gonna love that?

The vampire on *Being Human* worked as a hospital orderly to get free samples at the blood bank -- while rooming with a werewolf and an agoraphobic ghost.

It's all a *Father Knows Best* feel-good vibe with just enough action to get viewers coming back every week. But the basic message is that vampires and other things that go bump in the night are just subjugated minorities.

The hell they are! Dude, they're *dead*. They want to drink your blood and make you *dead*.

Dead is not good in the interests of going on living. Any of this penetrating your thick skull?

If we're not careful, the monsters are gonna take a piggy back ride on every other civil rights movement in the world and freaking integrate with those smooth-talking, aristocratic, well-educated vampires solidly leading the charge.

How's that for a juicy little spin on *Guess Who's Coming to Dinner?*

Bloodsucker Myth Confirmed

Vampires are hiding in plain sight and they have plenty of political ambitions. They have for centuries. Ever heard of the Borgias?

Uh yeah, Cesare and Lucrezia, which means vamps have made it to the halls of the Vatican. Think about it. What better way to get on top of vampire hunting than from the inside?

Get the attention firmly directed against witches and burn a lot of loud-mouthed women in the process. Score one for the paranormal patriarchy.

You think they just stopped doing that in the 18th century? Wrong. Their methods might have changed, but the bloodsuckers still have an agenda. Nothing has changed but the way they work the propaganda.

Chapter 2 - Pop Goes the Vampire

Don't get me wrong. I like a good vampire movie or book as well as the next living, breathing person. Problem is, that's where most people think they're getting accurate info on how to deal with the undead. Uh, dude, there's a reason that stuff is called "fiction."

Let's start with one of my pet peeves. There are so many, but I'm gonna pick werewolves. The real article is worse than a pack of coyotes in the neighborhood and damned annoying in their own right, but werewolves are not vampiric lap dogs.

Oh, dear Lord. I see that shocked look on your faces. You didn't know lycanthropes are real, too? How have you not been turned into hamburger yet? It's called cryptozoology people. Look it up, study, learn, and tell Bigfoot I said hi.

Nice guy. Could use some Odor Eaters, but a nice guy.

Moving on.

Monster Lodge Meetings Don't Exist

First, let me just get this off my many chest. Great jumping Jehoshaphat, save me from that fake *Twilight* load of crap! I can handle my vamps doing damn near anything except sparkling. I mean seriously, the whole idea is like the bastard love child of an Elton John concert and *Nosferatu*.

But the real issue here is this whole vampire / werewolf / Sharks / Jets thing Stephenie Meyer has got going in those books that people are now accepting while they debate which guy was sexier and more tragically misunderstood. Really?

It's just one step above *Abbot & Costello Meet Frankenstein*. Now, bro, seriously, I love that movie. It's got everything: Frankenstein, Dracula, the Wolfman -- the freaking Invisible Man even. But here's the paranormal rub. There is *zero* evidence even remotely suggesting those guys all belong to the same lodge hall.

If we want to stick purely with the dates all these stories first hit the popular perception, Bram Stoker's *Dracula* was published in 1897 and Mary Shelley came out with *Frankenstein* anonymously in 1823.

I get the whole creative urge to re-imagine stories that are getting on up toward 200 years old, but we gotta keep the fact and fiction separate.

Now, as for werewolf fiction, the "origin" story is a little harder to nail down. There were a lot of books floating around the 19th century Gothic horror scene. Let's just go with *Wagner the Wehr-Wolf* by G.W. M. Reynolds from 1847. It's the classic plot line:

- good guy
- deal with the devil
- youth and wealth in exchange for periodically going fuzzy
- you gotta kill people to get the good stuff

Just to make the English majors happy, this is also the same period Robert Louis Stevenson wrote *The Strange Case of Dr. Jekyll and Mr. Hyde* (1886), which is a decent spin on the werewolf transformation thing since Mr. Hyde a la Hollywood is usually in serious need of a shave and some decent dental work.

The "classic" werewolf as most people know him really dates from the 1941 Lon Chaney Jr. movie, *The Wolf Man* when the gypsy, deliciously played by Maria Ouspenskaya (who has like the best name *ever)* recites the classic curse:

Even a man who is pure in heart
And says his prayers by night
May become a wolf
When the wolfbane blooms
And the autumn moon is bright.

This is also where we get the common knowledge "silver bullet makes wolfie go bye-bye" wisdom. More on that shortly.

So, yeah, the popular writing on all this stuff is happening at the same time, but the *only* reason these dudes started hanging out together was because some studio head in the *20th century* stared at the numbers, saw that the individual movies brought in some decent box office, and decide to go ensemble cast in the name of profit.

Is there a whole paranormal society underlying our own? Damn straight there is, but they're not throwing a sorority mixer or having meet and greets. They deal with each other when necessary by the rules of their own cultures.

Bloodsucker Myth Busted

Vampires do not hang out with werewolves. They do not sew body parts back together and yell "It's alive!" at the camera. There is no vampire / werewolf turf war.

It will not, however, surprise me if I flip open the laptop some day and see an ad for Twilight: The Musical complete with some fanged chick doing a bad Rita Moreno imitation about how much she likes sucking blood in America.

Animal Control Meets Mind Control

Now, Laurell K. Hamilton does something kinda cool with the whole vamp / wolf thing in her Anita Blake books. Talk about monster porn! Geez. Ya gotta have graph paper to figure out who's doing what to who . . . and how . . . in those books. But I digress. Anita's main squeeze is a master vampire and he has an animal to call, the wolf.

Messy in the romance department since the wolf he calls is Anita's other main squeeze, Richard, the uptight leader of the local werewolf pack.

(Yeah. They apparently run in packs. Also a little off the canon there since your classic werewolf is solitary, tortured, and basically a whining pain in the ass when he's not ripping somebody's throat out.)

Anyway, you get the picture. The Anita Blake books are completely *menage a' fang*. But Hamilton has done her homework and strung things together with a little more realism than ole Steph "Sparkle" Meyer.

Really old vampires can control humans by staring into their eyes. So in theory, they could control animals the same way. In some traditions, vampires can only control nocturnal creatures, like wolves and bats, so Jean Claude in the Anita Blake books summoning a werewolf to do his bidding hangs together pretty well.

Bloodsucker Myth Confirmed

Really old vampires do have the ability to control the minds of humans with a form of mesmerism or hypnosis.

The scariest thing going on in those books though? Vampires campaigning for their civil rights. "I have a dream" gone straight to nightmare land.

Minor Movie / Book Detour

Okay, so I guess we're gonna have to talk vampire books and movies here whether I want to or not. I admit I read the Anita Blake books. Why? See previous reference re monster porn. But there's so much vampire fiction out there and so much more hitting the self-published air waves, it's hard to start a list.

Look, I'm not the mind police. Read whatever the hell you want to, just don't believe all of it much less take it as a primer for dealing with the undead. That's like my sainted mother calling *The National Enquirer* a newspaper. Only because that sorry rag is printed on newsprint paper and is suitable for puppies to pee on.

There's only three other book series I've dipped into:

- The Sookie Stackhouse novels by Charlaine Harris. Pretty good stuff and I like the little extra Louisiana-Marie Laveau-voodoo *thing* she's got going there.

- It's gotten kinda cliche, but it's a classic, so yeah, *Interview with the Vampire* by Anne Rice. Hated the (1994) movie. — Now stop. Don't get your tighty whities in a twist. Brad and Tom just set my teeth on edge. Make Angie a vampire and you'll get my attention. — But the books are a decent refresh of the whole basic vampire myth. Interestingly enough, Rice is from Louisana and Harris is right next door in Mississippi. Lot of inspiration back in the bayou.

- Tanya Huff's "Blood" books starting with *Blood Price* are worth your time. Who couldn't love a vampire who is the bastard son of Henry VIII? And his cop friend Vicki Nelson is pretty kick ass, especially when they start exchanging platelets.

I read one of the *Twilight* books and pretty much hurled it across the room.

You want a real hardcore how-do-I-make-it when-the-vampire-shit hits the fan novel? Go find yourself a copy of *I Am Legend* by Richard Matheson and then watch all three film versions:

- 1964 - *The Last Man on Earth* - Vincent Price

- 1971 - *The Omega Man* - Charlton Heston (Which is like a trip back to 1969, baby.)
- 2007 - *I Am Legend* - Will Smith

My pick of the litter? *The Last Man on Earth*. The nerd vamp beating on the front door (complete with mirror and garlic) and taunting Vincent Price. Classic.

It's hardly a complete movie list, but I'd definitely go with:

- **The Hunger** (1983) - Catherine Deneuve and Susan Sarandon getting it on. Need I say more?

- **The Lost Boys** (1987) - Real character driven friendship meets the dark side story with Kiefer Sutherland sporting one of the great bleached blonde looks of all time.

- **Bram Stoker's Dracula** (1992) - Mainly I just want Gary Oldman's cool glasses. This one is so overdone and pompous, I love it and Anthony Hopkins as Van Helsing is icing on the red velvet cake.

- **From Dusk Till Dawn** (1996) - This one is like a telenovela meets Dracula in a Mexican strip club. You don't even know it's a freaking vampire movie until better than half way through and then it's game on!

- **Abraham Lincoln Vampire Hunter** (2012) - Kind of a fan of alternate history here a la Harry Turtledove. Love the ax, and the paranormal twist on the Civil

War. It's one of my new favorites.

But here's the thing people, you gotta take this stuff for what it is — entertainment. You want to look at it as hard core vampirology? You are seriously missing the boat.

Chapter 3 - Vamp History 101

How have vampires managed to hide in plain sight for centuries and work on realizing their political ambitions? Obfuscation. Yeah, look at me. I know big words.

Obfuscation is one of those hard-to-understand words that means . . . drum roll, please . . . hard to understand.

That's what vamps are all about. They make things hard to understand, whether it's what they're saying to you when they turn on the creepy mind control crap, or the real story on what they're doing up late after grave time.

Let's take a little field trip.

Greek Mythology: The Lamia

If you go with Greek mythology, the first vampire was created because Zeus couldn't keep it in his pants. He had an affair was a Libyan princess named Lamia who was either Poseidon's daughter or granddaughter. Those Greek gods were kinda loosey goosey on the family tree thing.

Anyway, Zeus did have a significant other, Hera, and I don't know too many old ladies who are down with their guys stepping out.

Of course, in typical chick fashion, Hera had to take it out on Lamia. Kidnapped her, killed all the kids she had by Zeus, and then drove her into exile. Lamia didn't have the power to really strike back so, in the next round of pass-the-buck bingo, she started attacking humans by stealing babies and sucking the life out of their mothers.

As the story developed, "Lamia" turned into an unearthly legion with fashion sense that was hard to pull off. The top half of their body was female and human. The bottom half? Snake. The lamia suck the blood from children and use the life force to make themselves look all pretty so they can lead young men astray, as in dead.

The ancient Greeks were down with the bloodsucking thing. They had a minor deity called Mormo who also went after kids, but then Christianity came to town and we start hearing about the vrykolakas -- demons of the undead who get up out of the dirt and start dishing out the misery.

The Greek Orthodox Church latched on to all kinds of reasons about why somebody would take a postmortem walk, but basically the stories all boiled down to don't be all bad and sinful and you won't be waking up in the casket six feet under with a major case of the A-positive munchies. The solution for a suspected vrykolakas was to dig them up and burn what was left of them to ash.

Let's just look at the Cliff's Notes version of this one vampire legend.

- created due to a betrayal / sin
- motivated by blood vengeance
- powered / protected by deception

Sorry, I'm not getting the sensitive, misunderstood, in need of a Vampire Bill of Rights vibe here.

The eggheads figure Greek mythology, which has some basis in factual events, dates from 900-800 BC. But let's take things a little farther back, like to the Creation. (Apologies to the evolutionists. You'll get your say here in a minute.)

And God Made Woman Version 1.0

According to the ancient Jewish texts, God kinda went with a do-over when he made woman. Even though she's gotten slammed for centuries on the original sin thing, Eve wasn't the first chick to buck the all-male establishment. That would be Lilith.

See, the first time around, God made Adam and Lilith both from the Earth, as in equal -- a little detail Lilith grabbed on to fast. She refused to be subservient to Adam in bed and basically blew the Garden of Eden pop stand to go give birth to her own kids.

God sent three angels out to haul her back and when she said no, they went all murderous on her and starting knocking off a hundred of her kids a day to get her to obey the Big Guy.

Lilith turned into a child killer herself and morphed into a winged night demon with claws. She was one bad bitch, but she also had seductive powers, coming to men at night to drain their life force.

Technically that makes her a succubus, but those gals are close cousins of vampires. Both suck out life force, one in the form of blood and the other as life spirit, what the Chinese call chi and what we might call the soul. Either way, take too much and there's nothing but a corpse left.

Know Your Suckage

A succubus is a female demon who seduces men and draws off their life force or chi during sex. They can either take a guy out with one big massive, er, bang, or they can feed repeatedly and let you die a slow, but oh-so-pleasurable death.

The male counterpart is called an incubus. Neither a succubus nor an incubus is a revenant like a vampire, and vampires aren't the only revenants.

What's a Revenant?

Obviously vampires aren't the only creatures that return from the dead to walk among the living. Zombies fit the same profile. "Revenant" is just a fancy term for the re-animated dead. Especially in the world of fiction, there's all kinds of vehicles for having dead folks up walking around.

Before Anita Blake was a vampire executioner in the Laurell K. Hamilton books she was a necromancer, a person who could raise the dead, usually for a price to find out where Daddy hid the will.

At least the way Hamilton writes it, the corpses, which I guess are technically zombies, wake up, don't know they're dead, answer some questions, and then they're put back in the ground. If, however, they're kept up and about too long, they do start to rot like your classic zombies.

See how much fun the writers can have manipulating this stuff to pull off a plot device, and why a good story is not a source of factual research? Yes, I'm repeating myself, because I'm still not sure you're listening.

Emotional Vampires

A few years back the self-help gurus were talking a lot about emotional vampires, and then the feel-good-du-jour attention was directed on to something new. Thing is, that emotional vampire stuff was really on point.

If you have a lot of supernatural critters feeding on sex, sooner or later some DNA is gonna get swamped and little half-supernatural babies will come into the world.

Maybe those kids aren't full-blown one thing or the other, which is the curse of all hybrids, but they can still feed on the rest of us in more subtle ways.

Emotional vampires have the ability to throw you off your emotional center by striking at your self-worth.

- "Wow! Aren't you lucky you're the kind of person who can get away with a few extra pounds."

- "I would never have the courage to wear that! Aren't you special?"

- "Don't be so sensitive. What happened to your sense of humor?"

Call it defining someone else, gas lighting, or out and out verbal abuse, but emotional vampires have the power to elicit negative emotions and then feed on them like the rest of us pig out on carbs.

They might not technically be part of the "monster," set, but they don't use their abilities for good and you need to stay the hell away from them.

When you're around somebody and your mood suddenly plummets, you feel suddenly anxious, depressed, or worried? You're around one of these lesser vamps and they're feeding on you!

Tip of the Ice Berg

So, the Ancient Greeks and the pre-Eden tale of Lilith are just two examples of vampire origin myths. You can go culture by culture around the world and come up with all kinds of stories with elements of the now classic vampire:

- The vetalas of India inhabit corpses and hang upside down from trees near cemeteries.

- In 12th century Hungary church inquisitors interrogated a pagan tho claimed to have called forth a blood drinking demon called an izcacus.

- Romanian folklore offers up the moroi, strigoli, and pricolici, all of whom drank blood or had other vampiric qualities.

- The Romani people or gypsies believe in revenants called mullo who cause malicious acts and drink the blood of the living.

- In the Scottish highlands there are legends of a creature much like a succubus called the Baobhan sith, as well as the Lhiannan Shee, a fairy spirit with vampire-like habits.

- On Madagascar the Besileo people believe in a vampire called the ramanga.

And let us not forget the Mexican goat killing blood sucking chupacabra.

'Cause really, can you write any kind of book about the paranormal and not find a place somewhere for the chupacabra?

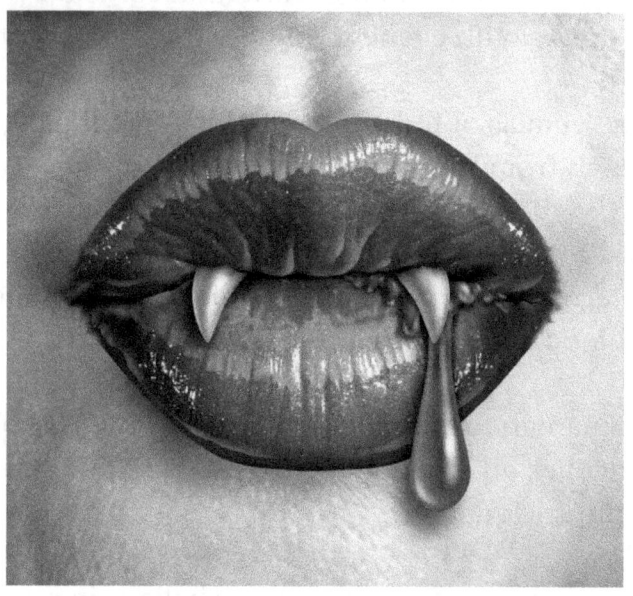

Let's just take a big ole leap here and say if you can find stories about vampires in every culture in the world, exactly why are we still doing the "are they real" thing?

I'm sick unto death of people just taking shortcuts on the history and going straight to Vlad the Impaler. Yes, he did inspire Bram Stoker to write *Dracula* and yes, he was a bad dude. Best estimate, Vlad offed about 100,000 people. But was he a vampire? Uh, no.

And neither was the Blood Countess, Elizabeth Bathory. She did like to torture young girls and she did bathe in the blood of her victims because she thought it would keep her young. Some accounts also say she drank the blood as well, but hey, Cruella de Vil wanted to kill puppies. Vain bitches, yes. Vampires, no.

If you're going to defend yourself from evil, you have to accept that it comes in many flavors, including human.

Let's Clarify Some Language

It might be easier to come up with a big all-purpose evil, but then you can't see the forest for the stakes. Evil comes in many different forms and that can affect how you respond to it.

Diabolical Evil

The church (as in organized Christian religion) actually sticks with a fairly chocolate and vanilla interpretation. On the one hand you have God and the angels, divine good while on the other it's Satan and all his demons.

That falls under the heading of diabolical evil and the whole set-up more or less fell in place after the War in Heaven when Satan fell from grace.

Most Christians believe that Satan is actively at work in the world trying to severe their relationship with God via any means available to him including a whole host of demons, minions, and other agents.

There's a lot of vampire fiction that suggests the bloodsuckers are in league with the devil, but no real evidence to suggest they're Satan's agents. My personal take is that vampires fall under the more "scientific" heading of "monster."

Monsters

"Monsters" are any kind of beings that go against the order of nature. That's why they're called "supernatural." It's not natural for a man to turn into a wolf when the moon comes up. It's not natural to sew body parts together, zap them with lighting, and get a reanimated patchwork corpse.

Most folks would agree it's not natural for one creature to drink the blood of another even in the name of balanced nutrition.

Vamps may just be eating to stay alive, but they're doing it in a way that goes against nature for the simple reason that they look like humans, they sound like humans, and they were once humans.

I'm getting ready to share my own theory with you that vampires are another species altogether — so I'm kinda with Darwin on this one. But traditionally, vampires are lumped in with the monsters.

Bad Humans aka Serial Killers

Guys like Vlad the Impaler and chicks like Elizabeth Bathory? Those are serial killers, people. The Jeffrey Dahlmers of another century. Yeah, they're evil. What they do sure as hell is monstrous, but they're bad *humans*.

Not to ruin your day or anything, but not all the monsters are actually monsters, some of them are just your neighbors — and some of those folks are twisted enough even the vampires leave them alone.

Pound for pound, *Dexter* scared me a hell of a lot more than *True Blood* ever did.

How Are Vampires Really Made?

Kinda sounds like a line out of *The Godfather*. Made men with fangs. The answer to this question, in practical terms, is pretty much like the sex talk from hell with your mother.

There are tons of theories about the origin of vampires and tons of theories about how little vampires are made.

- A dog or a cat jumped over your body after you died. (Look, I didn't say they were *good* theories, I'm just giving you the list.)

- You're a witch and you didn't do what the Catholic Church told you to do, so you die and go all bloodsucker. (Which confuses the hell out of me, because how is that damnation when your "go to hell" ticket is already punched for the witchcraft thing?)

- You commit suicide.

- You're possessed by a demon.

- You're a fallen angel. (Little case of grandiosity there, dead dude?)

Frankly, I think all of those are pretty freaking silly. I'm going with:

- You've been bitten by a vampire.

- A vampire swapped some blood with you.

- You're a dhampir, half-human half-vampire because your folks did the nasty and figured the vamp's little swimmers were no good. That's usually how it works, male vamp / female human. The vamp just has to feed first to get his, er, systems going.

How Do You Stop Vamps from Rising?

With the exception of the dhampir thing, you gotta pretty much die and rise to be a vampire, so there's all kinds of whacky burial-based strategies to keep that from happening:

- When a person kicks, you stop all the clocks in the house to literally stop time until you can get the body buried in consecrated ground.

- Cover up all the mirrors so they don't take the dead person's soul.

- Be buried face down in consecrated ground. (No idea on this one unless they figure if you decide to get up out of the grave they can at least get you pointed in the wrong direction.)

- Bury the corpse with iron and garlic and/or put scythes near the grave to keep demons away.

- Get an undertaker who also happens to be a witch and let her put some mojo on the grave.

But seriously? If you really think somebody is gonna get up out of the grave and do the Dracula, there's only four option in my book:

- Stake the corpse in the casket before you close the lid.
- Cut the head off.
- Burn the body.
- Scatter the ashes to the four winds or put them in a burlap bag and toss the bag into running water.

If you're a safety man go with stake, decapitate, light'er up — in that order. If you're really into redundant slaying strategies, stuff some garlic bulbs in the mouth after decapitation and before burning.

In the American South, it's still not unheard of to stop the clocks when someone dies and to cover the mirrors, but it's also pretty traditional to sit up with the body for three days and nights.

Nowadays folks think they're showing respect, but this one is straight out of African-American folklore. What you're doing is waiting for grandma to sit up out of the casket so you can put her back down again.

Takes three days for a vampire to rise, so why go to the trouble of planting the corpse until the waiting period is over?

Do You Have a Theory Rex?

Why thank you for asking. Yes, I do have a theory. I've been reading this stuff for a long time and dude, it did not start with Bram Stoker digging up the Vlad the Impaler legend and writing *Dracula* in 1897. There's talk of some form of vampire all the way back to the Garden of Eden.

Now look, I honestly don't care if you're religious or not, and, as much as I hate to break it to you, crosses don't reliably repel vampires. More on that later, but if you're on eBay shopping for a silver crucifix you might want to hold your next bid.

Let's go back to Darwin for a second. First off, Darwin didn't say squat about survival of the fittest the way most people think of it. He just said the animals that have the qualities that help them survive get together with others like themselves and make little animals that will survive.

The best adapted traits get passed on because those are the creatures staying alive to pass them on. It's not really all that complicated. I think vampires have been with us since we climbed up out of the ooze or got made from the dirt or however the hell it happened. Theologically I don't freaking care.

The church plays a big ole role in the whole body of vampire literature and myth, but the answer is a heck of a lot older. I think vampires look like us, sound like us, live in our world, and like every other creature, they can survive by reproduction.

But instead of taking a roll in the hay with a lady vamp --
which they will do by the way -- they primarily make more
of their own kind by infecting a victim with their own
blood. As I've said before, I may or may not know
somebody who works at the CDC, who may or may not be
doing a serological study of vamp blood.

If I did know somebody, I could tell you that vampire
blood is a lot like human blood but it doesn't replenish
itself. We make our own blood to keep our bodies going.
Vamps have to get their blood from an outside source.
Their hearts don't beat because their blood doesn't
coagulate. For want of a better term it kinda swims through
their veins under its own power. No pump required.

As far as I know, no one has admitted to finding ancient
vampires in an archeological dig, but I think if they could
take every vampire on the earth and trace his lineage
backwards, they'd find one "original."

Whatever happened to that proto-vamp that zapped him
up from the dead, he woke up with a hunger for blood and
the ability to make others of his own kind and from that
one accident of nature, a parallel race was born.

There aren't as many of them as there are of us, but
vampires live longer and are arguably better designed than
we are. I don't know why some vampires also have the
ability to get human women pregnant, but they do, which
is why we have half-bloods called dhampirs.

Also called "daywalkers," there's frankly a lot less known

about just how many of these hybrids are walking among us. They have all the powers inherited from the male vampire, but none of the usual weaknesses, which, if you think about it, may make them even scarier than Daddy Dearest.

After all, genetics does give us the theory of hybrid vigor. The offspring of two different species is healthier and stronger in most cases than either of the parents.

We do know that dhamiprs are not immortal per se, but they do age very, very slowly. Are they in league with the vampires? Hard to tell, but simply by existing in the no-man's land between the two cultures, dhampirs may be a hidden threat in their own right.

But, one monster at a time. Once you accept that evolution gave the vampire a radically different circulatory system, it's not difficult to believe that other things about him are pretty different, too. Hence the set of superpowers — enhanced senses, physical speed, mesmerism, mind control and all that other stuff.

Vampires are another version of us. In their minds, they're a better version of mankind and we're their prime food source. Sorry if this offends the vegans among us, but dude, as far as a vamp is considered, you're just a juicy steak on the hoof.

So this idea of curing a vampire? Cure him of what, exactly? Being what he's supposed to be? That's like saying if they'd just tried to cure the shark in *Jaws* there would have been no reason for the God-awful sequels.

Let me put that a little more directly. Do you really think you're gonna have any luck getting a great white shark to go vegan?

What Can Vampires Really Do?

There's a lot of speculation about vampire "super powers," but I'm going with pretty much the classics because they get proven over and over again.

- Some form of mind control, usually with a compelling stare that mesmerizes the victim. This usually extends to actually reading thoughts and maybe even being able to see into the future.

- The ability to shapeshift. The standard is the vamp turns into a bat, but you'll run into accounts of them actually becoming wolves or other creatures.

- Control or influence over animals or elements of nature, like being able to call up a thunderstorm.

- Heightened physical abilities for speed, strength, flying, night vision, hearing, smell — pretty much everything we can do they can do *better*.

Vampires also heal really well, and they can create more vampires either to build their power base or just because they're lonely. So are they introverts or extroverts? Uh, yeah, both.

Remember, vampires are immortal, so sometimes they'll be off living the whole lone hunter lifestyle and sometimes they're congregating in nests. Just depends on the master plan. Beware of both. You got a vamp going all Unibomber, that's a problem. You got a bunch of vamps going all *Lord of the Flies*, that's a problem.

Chapter 4 - How to ID a Vampire

Don't come out of the gate thinking you can predict what a vampire can and can't do because it depends on the vamp you're dealing with. Even if it does make the religious types go bonkers, vampires really are born again.

When they come back, they get a second set of natural talents. Those abilities do fall within a set of potential powers, but the combinations and strengths vary from one individual to the next.

So, how do you know if you're dealing with a vampire?

- Redheads have always fallen under suspicion because Judas Iscariot was a redhead and some traditions make him one of the first vampires.

- Watch out for anyone claiming super light sensitivity, as in they never leave their house until the sun goes down and all the windows are covered up.

- Claims of chronic anemia are pretty suspect, especially if no doctor is involved and the person has a miraculous overnight "improvement" that disappears as quickly as it showed up. Also beware if the person in question never eats in front of you.

- Clearly these last two would explain pale skin. Forget the whole pointy fingernails and ear tips thing. Not true.

- Lots of "experts" claim vampires are obsessive compulsive and have this silly notion that if you throw a bunch of seeds at one he'll have to stop coming after you to stop and count the seeds. Yeah, okay Monk, bet your jugular on that load of crap.

  The OCD thing also has a Christian link to Judas, claiming vampires are the greedy descendants of the man who betrayed Christ for 30 pieces of silver. If you go with this interpretation, however, you have to throw coins at the vamp.

- Vampire don't cast a shadow (this is pure Bram Stoker and may not stand up in real life) and they have no reflection in any shiny surface, not just a mirror.

They also won't come into a home unless they receive a direct invitation (which you can rescind later on, by the way, but plan on tacking some protection spells on top of the "not welcome" sign just to be sure.)

Vampire Physiology

Not surprisingly, there's not a lot of vampires rolling up their sleeves and agreeing to be lab rats, but there are some things we can conclude about vampire physiology from centuries of reports and observations:

- **Eternal youth.** The vampire stays the same "age" at least in physical appearance for the rest of his "undead" life. His hair doesn't grow or change color, piercings don't heal, tattoos don't fade. His abilities are better and stronger, but physically he's the same.

  Only when vampires are several centuries old can you see a change and then it's kinda like the weight of experience, not age. Old vampires are really still, like creepy intense. They've seen it all and nothing impresses them anymore.

- **Differing bite levels.** Vampires control the effect of their bites, either feeding on, draining, or turning their victims. Since there is no other real way for vampires to reproduce, a vamp makes a clear cut decision about "fathering" offspring.

  In vampire fiction that's a whole set up for a life-long relationship between a vampire and his "sire" or "maker." Those connections are supposed to form the basis for clans or nests of vampires.

- **Selective feeding**. Vampires also feed selectively to make sure they're getting the good stuff. They don't just want healthy blood, they want smart blood. Victim profiles suggest vamps like the twenty-something crowd, preferably educated and with some class.

  A vamp isn't going to turn some white-trash schmuck and ruin the neighborhood. Bloodsuckers are elitist as hell, so they prefer to snack on fellow elites. Think of it as a supernatural country club.

- **Cross-species feeding**. It is possible for a vampire to feed on other species, like cattle or horses, to get blood when they're desperate. There's no chance of the animal going vamp and this is just a total emergency feed on the part of the vamp. The blood doesn't give the vamp the same quality "nutrition" and it probably tastes like hell, tool!

- **Pale and lean.** Vampires are almost always pale skinned because they stay just mildly anemic. If they're hungry, they really do look like death warmed over. They also tend to be lean and muscular, suggesting all of their blood nutrition goes to pure energy conversion to support their enhanced abilities.

- **Magnesium dependent**. Research suggests that the most important component vampires draw from blood is not iron, but magnesium. Their circulatory system is more efficient and flexible and their blood does not coagulate.

  They also don't react to temperature and can withstand great climate extremes with no ill effect. When humans don't get enough magnesium, they get irritable, angry, and anxious, which is how vamps start acting when they're really hungry.

- **Non-functioning organs**. Vampires do need oxygen on some level, but their respiration doesn't seem to have anything to do with the lungs. They may derive oxygen from the blood they drink, but their needs are at a bare minimum. In fact, none of a vampires organs really work after the vamp has been turned.

The heart doesn't beat, but it's still the center of the circulatory system, which is why a stake to the heart works, but not the way it would with us. It doesn't kill the vampire, it puts him in suspended animation.

- **Living blood**. Vampire blood is alive in its own right. Again, there is no coagulation. Once the blood is in the vampire's veins, it doesn't need the heart to move it through the circulatory system. The stuff swims on its own.

  That's one thing most of the movies get right. You know that "through the microscope" shot at the vampire blood being all weird and over active? It's true.

- **Spontaneous wound healing**. Unless a wound is inflicted with a silver implement, healing is almost spontaneous for any external wound. You can unload a .9 mil in a vamp's chest and he'll keep coming right at you.

  It may take him a few days to completely heal and he'll need a good meal, but bullets alone won't take him down for the count. Some research says part of the reason is that a vamp's whole system is geared toward preserving its blood content until the next feed, so they've got vasoconstriction down to an art.

Immortality is Hard to Pull Off

Make no mistake. Vampires go to great lengths to hide their

activities. Contrary to popular myth, they don't actually go on bloody killing sprees if they can avoid it. That kind of stuff attracts way too much attention, especially now when everyone has a camera in their cellphone.

Having groupies who are willing donors makes life a lot easier for vampires, and many have reconciled themselves to living, at least in part, on blood obtained from more discreet sources — like blood banks. It's even been suggested that some of the biggest blood banks are actually owned by powerful vampires who quietly skim off the liquid profits.

When you have a really old and entrenched vampire, he's someone who has re-invented himself a number of times — and has the money to pull it off again and again. Vampires often present themselves as the younger relatives of some elderly recluse who died childless. This is a good story to hide the uncanny physical resemblance since the vamp is actually just impersonating himself.

To avoid suspicion, vampires rarely stay in one location more than a few years at a time. They keep different households and separate identities around the world, blending in and out of communities and social circles with ease.

When anyone does question any inconsistencies in a vampire's story, a healthy dose of mesmerism generally solves the problem, or the person doing the asking simply meets an untimely demise.

Human Retainers

It is common for vampires to form human alliances that continue through generations of human servants. Rarely are these servants actually sources of blood. Instead, they are valued facilitators, motivated by extreme loyalty to their masters, whom they will protect at all costs. As much as I hate to admit it, vampires can have human friends.

Friendship is a difficult thing to define under most circumstances, and who the hell knows why a vamp decides *not* to chow down on someone, but it happens. Don't mistake a vampire's human retainer for some stumbling moron named Igor. That's not the kind of human a vamp will befriend, much less trust with his life and secrets.

If a human is in the service of a vampire, expect that human to be as dangerous as, or more dangerous than his master. Don't cross him (or her) and never make him think you present a threat to his favorite vamp.

Chapter 5 - Vampire Protection Strategies

Okay, now we're getting down to the stake carving. You've accepted the fact that they're out there. You're over the cool factor, and now you want to do something to protect yourself.

Garlic

If you go the garlic (*allium sativum*) route, your social life is over. I'm just saying, since you have to wear the garlic around your neck and hang it around all the entrances to your house.

Garlic doesn't actually do anything bad to the vampire, it just makes you and your place stink. Since all the vampire's senses are heightened, they just don't like to eat a meal that absolutely reeks.

I wouldn't count on garlic stopping a really hungry

vampire, but as a first layer of protection, it's okay to go ahead and include this one in your arsenal.

The garlic has to be fresh, however, and don't be a total tool and sprinkle garlic powder around because in that case, you're so stupid, you deserve whatever happens to you.

Grow Your Own Garlic

Not being the gardening type, I asked one of my more Martha-Steart-esque friends to give us the 411 on growing your own garlic. Here's the instructions. Sounds pretty simple to me, but I kill air plants, so I'm no judge.

Garlic plants like full-out sun and will grow almost anywhere. Your best bet for home cultivation is raised beds so you get good drainage. Plant in the fall. Every clove will produce a new bulb. Soak them in water first with a tablespoon of baking soda and a tablespoon of liquid seaweed from your garden store.

Place the pointed end of the clove up and cover with 2 inches of dirt. Space them 6-8 inches apart. Cover the bed with 6 inches of dried grass clippings or leaves. In 4-8 weeks, shoots will start to push through the mulch. Leave the covering material in place into spring to keep the weeds down and conserve moisture.

Garlic plants go dormant until spring when they need about an inch of water per week. Stop watering in June or when the leaves start to get yellow. That's when the bulbs begin to get firm.

In June the plants put on flowery tops that straighten out into stalks or scapes. Cut those back to encourage bulb growth. When about 75% of the leaves turn yellow-brown, usually in early July, you can start digging up the bulbs. Dig, don't pull!

Tie the bulbs together in groups of 6-10 and hang them in a shady, dry, ventilated area to cure for 4-6 weeks. Then trim off the roots and store the garlic in recycled mesh onion bags.

For optimal storage, place the garlic in an area with a temperature of 55-60 degrees F. Once a garlic bulb is broken, the individual cloves remain pungent for 7-10 days. Fresh whole garlic bulbs will last 3-6 months.

Don't store garlic in the refrigerator. The cold only adds moisture that leads to faster deterioration from mold growth. Freezing changes the consistency and flavor of garlic and is not recommended for cooking.

But hey, you're not going to be feeding garlic to the vampires. You just need the odor, so freeze away. If you're hanging garlic over your windows and doors, you're going to need a lot, so growing your own and storing as much as possible is a good plan.

Other Useful Plants

Garlic gets all the press, but there are a lot of plants you can use in and around your house to protect yourself and/or actually put down a vamp. Basically, you can do some very effect vampire-proofing around the house just by making good landscaping choices.

- Plant **blackthorn** (*Prunus spinosa*) shrubs around your home and sew blackthorn into your clothing. Blackthorn is a small tree that reaches a maximum height of about 16 feet / 5 meters.

  The bark is blackish and the branches are very stiff and kind of spiny. It's not a bad looking tree, putting out white flowers and a fruit called a "sloe." The trees are native to Europe, western Asia, and northwest Africa, but they'll grow in the eastern parts of North America.

- Hang **buckthorn** branches at gates and other entrances to keep out all forms of the walking dead. There are about 150 species of this plant in the genus *Rhamnus*. All of them are either big shrubs or small trees that are native to east Asia and North America. Far as I can tell, they all work to repel vampires.

- Place **dog rose vines** (*Rosa canina*) in coffins and on the grave to prevent the dead from rising. Dog rose is a climbing wild rose found in Europe, the northwest portions of Africa, and western Asia.

  The flowers are pale pink with some white and yellow stamens in the center. Dog rose has a lot of uses in traditional medicine, including as a treatment for viral infections, which may explain why the vamps don't like it.

- Hang **holly** from doors and windows. Again, lots of choices on this one. There are between 400-600 species of the stuff. Holly has been used metaphysically for centuries, going all the way back to the druids.

  It's a favorite wood for witches to use for their wands, and putting the stuff around the house keeps all kinds of little magic critters out of the woodwork. Be careful with the berries though; they're poisonous to humans and pets.

- Keep **juniper** in the house. Ditto on the mystical properties of juniper, or *Juniperus communis*. Witches use juniper incense to banish anything that can be bad for your health, so vampires definitely qualify.

  One thing you have to be careful about though. When you burn juniper, you can either purify the house (smudging) or accidentally cause something to manifest. If you're already dealing with a vampire, the last thing you need to do is summon a demon by accident.

- Fasten **mayflower** flowers and leaves to doors. Mainly when you're talking mayflower, the reference is to *Epigaea repens*, which is native to the eastern part of North America. It's a small creeping shrub with small white or pink flowers.

  If you're in England and you see a reference to mayflower, they're probably talking about hawthorn. Both are good to repel vampires.

- Plant fragrant roses around the house and keep the petals on hand as they are believed to burn a vampire's skin as bitterly as acid. Bury wild roses with bodies to prevent them from rising. Any kind of rose works, so you won't have any trouble finding something that will grow in your area.

Although wolfsbane (*Arnica montana*) is most often regarded as a protection against werewolves, it will also help to keep vampires out if placed above the doors of a house. The stuff grows all over Europe, but it's not native to the British Isles or the Balkan or Italian Peninsulas.

The plant contains the toxin helenalin, which is what is believed to work against both werewolves and vampires, but don't go chewing on wolfsbane yourself and wear gloves when you're working with it since it will cause skin irritation.

Silver

Until recent times the use of silver as a means of protection has been more closely associated with werewolf lore, but silver packs a lot of metaphysical power. I wear silver jewelry. Manly silver jewelry, but jewelry all the same.

Silver is considered to be the metal of the moon. It has calming and balancing properties and protects the wearer against negativity, reflecting away evil intentions.

All of these properties are magnified on a full moon, hence the use with werewolves, but silver is also useful against all forms of black magic and sorcery and as a protective agent with a vampire.

If you wound a vampire with a knife, stake, or any kind of projectile made of silver, the wound heals slowly or maybe not at all. Get the silver through the vamp's heart and it's game over.

Silver nails in the coffin lid help to keep a potential vampire from rising and if you're going to try to use a cross as a mean's of protection, you want one made of silver and preferably blessed by a priest.

Can You Get Silver Bullets?

Again, we're kinda over into werewolf territory here, but I have a lot of respect for the metaphysical powers of silver and you can wound a vampire pretty seriously with silver. Since I don't believe in getting any closer than necessary to something that wants to go after my jugular, I did look into the matter of silver bullets.

First off, in contradiction to my firm theory that you can find anything online, you can't actually go buy a box of silver bullets and it's not as easy to cast them up yourself as people make it look in the movies.

To make it work, you'll need to get your hands on a custom graphite mold designed to your specifications for the weapon you intend to use. Silver bullets return a great deal of inconsistency in casting. But if you can pull it off and get the bullets cast correctly, the rest of the reloading is standard.

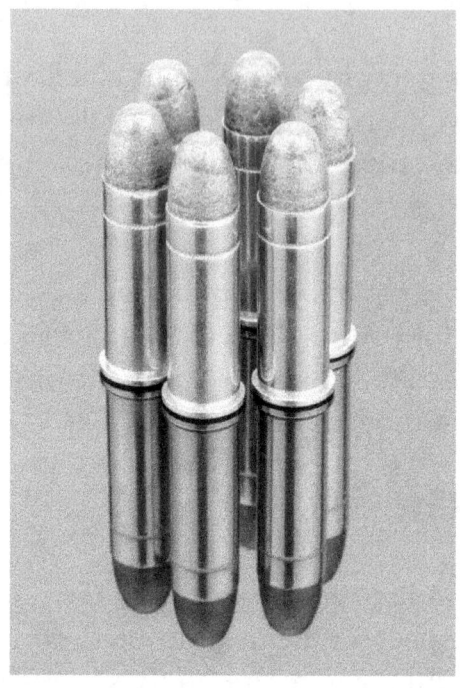

But frankly, after going crosseyed reading Michael Briggs' Article "Silver Bullets" at:

www.patriciabriggs.com/articles/silver/silverbullets.shtml

I'm gonna say this route is just too damned much trouble. If you're really serious about investigating this route, I'd look into tipping your bullets with silver.

I know it makes for good reading and viewing, but I'm not sold on a firearm as your best weapon against a vamp. They're just too fast and too impervious to injury with conventional weaponry. Now, ole Rex does have an alternate solution. Can you say incendiary rounds?

Remember what I said about mix and match strategy with vampires? Well, how about a .357 magnum loaded with 357 Mag Incendiary Fireball Ammo from Clark Custom Cartridge Company (clarkcustomcartridge.com)? They're pricey at $50 / £33.70 a box, but they'll light a vamp up like a Roman candle — and they'll shoot right through a steel plate.

Main problem here is that incendiary ammo is not legal in California, New York City, Chicago, Washington, D.C. and Massachusetts.

Not All Crosses Are Made Equal

The reasons I say a cross won't work reliably against a vampire is you have to be material specific. I always snort my Coke . . . uh, let me rephrase that . . . my soda always comes out of my nose when I see some movie moron making a cross with his fingers and driving a vampire back. Please.

If you're gonna use a cross and you don't have one made of silver, then you need aspen. That's the wood believed to have been used by the Romans to build the cross on which Jesus was crucified. No aspen? Go with ash, hawthorn, rowan, and linden. Some sources absolutely swear by white oak, but aspen and ash, from my research, seem to be the woods of choice.

There is absolutely no guarantee that crosses (or stakes) made out of any other material will work against a vampire, but they will probably piss him off good and proper.

Running Water

Legend holds that vampires can't cross running water except at the tide's ebb and flow. Folklore says the same is true of evil spirits, witches, and ghosts because water symbolizes purity, holiness, and the essence of life having the power to both cleanse and heal. In church ritual, water washes away sin and is the instrument of holy baptism.

In Greece, suspected vampires would be reburied on small islands so that the water would keep them imprisoned. In theory, you can chase a vampire into flowing water to kill him, but I gotta tell you, I don't have a lot of confidence in this one. The whole you can lead a horse to water thing.

Holy Water

Holy water is kind of a recent addition to the accepted canon of weapons against the undead. It's really popular in fiction. Buffy used the stuff constantly. The theory is pretty much the same as with garlic. Holy water burns the vampire, but it probably only works because the vamp thinks it will and because you think it will.

Yeah. That's the rub. Using holy water or any other article of faith means you gotta have faith. No belief, no protection. Plain as that. Doubt will get your ass killed, so make sure you take a pretty strong spiritual inventory before you rely on any holy item.

Your belief is probably the most crucial part, but it's to your advantage if the vampire was a Christian when he was alive. If the vampire knows all the religious beliefs associated with what he is and sees himself as damned, then he's gonna buy right into the whole cross-holy water-blessed object vibe and you're golden.

Thing is, vampires are becoming more and more secular right along with society, so if you have an atheist vampire and you're kinda on the fence? Well, I guess you could bless some water in the name of Madalyn Murray O'Hair and see what happens, but chances are you're just gonna have a wet vampire on your hands.

Issuing Invitations

Dude, it's pretty simple. If you don't want a vampire in your house, don't invite him in. If one does sneak in under the radar, however, you can formally un-invite him. That alone is an inconclusive strategy, however, so get the house blessed and use the plant protections discussed above.

You might also consider smudging the house with sage and even getting a white witch in to put up some protective wards. Just don't piss off the witch, or the vampire may be the least of your worries.

Salt is also associated with holiness and is often used to protect anyone summoning a spirit or to repel all kinds of evil in the form of demons, ghosts, and spirits. Especially in the case of rescinding an invitation, placing salt at the thresholds and on window sills is a good idea.

Use Lots of Mirrors

The more mirrors you have around the better. Vampires not only can't be seen in the mirror, but they really don't like the reflective surface and will try to break mirrors rather than have to be around them.

Ladies, I'm not saying you can drive a vampire back with your compact, but you can make one damned uncomfortable, maybe long enough that you can at least get away.

Mirror, Mirror on the Wall

Be careful when you're using a mirror. They've got a lot of metaphysical uses. The reason a vampire has no reflection in the mirror, according to most sources, is because he has no soul, which is what a mirror really shows us.

Now, if that is the case, most morning my soul has a wicked case of bed head and needs a shave and a cup of black coffee. But I digress.

Mirrors can act as gateways to other worlds. Do not test this theory by going in the bathroom and calling Bloody Mary. Just. Don't.

Mirrors can be used for divination, and they can induce visions. Don't get any bright ideas about trying some kind of incantation when you're using a mirror. Just hold it up, drive back the vamp, and get the hell out of there.

Destroying the Vampire's Resting Place

Man, we could argue for hours on this one. I don't actually subscribe to the idea that vampires sleep all day in coffins. I do think their powers are much weaker by day and that they prefer to be in dark spaces both for privacy and to protect themselves. If they sleep in coffins it's just because a casket is the ultimate blackout curtain.

Mortuary Trivia

Did you know there's actually a difference between a coffin and a casket? I got a drinking buddy who's an undertaker. A coffin is the old hexagonal or octagonal style where you nail the lid down. A casket is the high-dollar box they stiff us for and it can be locked. Now here's two questions for you. Why in the hell lock a dead man in a box and who in the hell keeps the key? I'm just saying.

The Native Soil Thing is a Myth

Also, that whole business about a vampire having to rest on his native soil? That's just a Bram Stoker plot device. Vamps do not ship containers of homeland potting soil around to survive. They are free to travel at will and don't have any mystical connection to the land of their origin.

It is likely that during the daylight hours they do live in rooms that are blacked out from sunlight, preferring to conduct their business at night.

This might have made them conspicuous in the days before the Internet, but now there are lots of people who don't leave home for days on end.

Technology has actually made it much, much easier for vampires to hide their longevity and re-create their identity every few years as need be.

The Value of the Mix and Match

Not a single one of these strategies is a magic bullet — not even the magic silver bullet. Don't be afraid to mix and match.

For instance, if you think a loved one is in danger of rising from the grave, and you're squeamish about the whole cutting off the head thing, then stake the corpse (or have it done), bury the body with dog rose vines and chain the coffin with silver.

And no, that's not a hard and fast formula. People. Use your imagination and the resources currently available!

The best stake for the job is the in your hand, but if all you have is a pocket mirror and some salt, go for it. This is about *survival*. Learn all the techniques and use what you have.

Stake du Jour

When in doubt, go with a classic. Let's talk stakes: design and use. First off, and all apologies to Buffy, a stake in the heart does not make a vampire conveniently crumble into a nice little pile of dust.

A stake to the heart will stop a vampire, but it doesn't kill him. If somebody else comes along and pulls the stake out, the vampire revives. That's why you've got to go to the next level and decapitate the bloodsucker, or at the very least chain them in the coffin with silver.

We've already gone over the best choices for wooden crosses. Same holds true for stakes: aspen, ash, hawthorn, rowan, and linden. That's in order of preference.

Tipping the stakes with silver is a good idea as well, not only because it adds a little extra protective mojo, but it reinforces the tip of the stake.

Now, if we take our cues from Buffy, when it comes time to actually use the stake, you do some nice kickboxing moves and stab for the heart — which will get you killed in nothing flat. You are a normal person not the chosen slayer, so get over yourself and get practical.

Jamming a wooden stake in the center of a vamp's ribcage, aiming correctly, missing ribs, and penetrating deeply enough to puncture the heart is harder than it sounds and it sounds plenty hard enough.

The classic Van Helsing move is to position the stake over an immobilized vampire and pound it home with a nice big mallet.

Crossbows Trump Mallets

Most people don't carry stakes and mallets, and anybody with half a functioning brain cell isn't going to want to get that close to a vampire, so I'm saying go with a crossbow.

And no, you're not gonna go full out Daryl Dixon / Walking Dead because no way in hell you're ever gonna be that cool and you know it. Get yourself a crossbow pistol and practice like there's no tomorrow.

I recommend a self-cocking, 80 lb. model. Get something with a metal body because there's a lot of plastic crap out there. You're looking to spend anywhere from $50 to $100 (£33.70-£67.40) to get something good.

Probably maximum range with a weapon like that is about 70 feet (21.33 meters). Obviously the closer you are, the better the penetrating power.

But here's the thing, that vampire isn't going to just stand there and wait to get staked. They move so damn fast, you blink and they're somewhere else. Don't go for a long shot. Get as close as you can for maximum penetrating velocity and a chance of actually getting your shot in before the vamp rockets out of the way.

One advantage you have is that vampires are arrogant. Once the bloodsucker sees that you're armed, he'll start pulling that mind control crap. That's a huge "danger Will Robinson" moment for you.

Resisting Mind Control

There is no fair fight with a vampire. They don't need to slip you a roofie — they *are* a roofie. Do not, under any circumstances, look a vampire straight in the eye. If you have the faith to use a holy object you can push the vampire back and blunt the impact of his stare. Ditto with using a mirror.

If you don't have faith in a holy object or in holy water, I think the important thing is really just breaking the vamp's concentration long enough to buy yourself an opportunity. This is totally off canon, but using mace or pepper spray right in those hypnotic eyes will get you a reaction. Maybe just a few seconds, but that can be more than enough time to pull the trigger on your cross bow.

I say go with a Mace Pepper Gun for distance defense to the eyes. You hold the thing just like a pistol, so you get better accuracy, plus you can use water cartridges to practice. It's $60 / £40.44 well spent since you can also use it on the living if the need arises. Two pack of refills, $18.99 / £12.80. Check'em out at mace.com.

Holy Water Dispersal Systems

Ideally if you're gonna go with holy water, you'd be able to get it in a pressurized canister like the refills for the pepper gun. I admit I haven't fiddle with this, because I actually have this thing about protective talismans, so I'm good with a silver cross. It's a no-atheists-in-foxholes mentality for me. You pray as much as I have clutching a cross while trying to save your ass and the thing has to have mojo.

Now, aside from doing a DYI thing there, go shopping for the most powerful (non-leaking) water pistol you can find. You really don't need power when you're dispersing holy water, but you do need distance. Spend at least $25 / £16.85 or you'll get a piece of crap.

Chapter 6 - Anti-Vampire Toolbox

Before we talk about putting something together that you can carry around, I asked one of my egghead buddies to give us the low down on antique vampire kits that come up for auction from time to time.

He's taking the real academic approach here, so don't think I've gone schizophrenic in the next section. I'm just copying and pasting from his email.

Seriously, what are these mainstream straights gonna say? "Yeah, the monsters are out there and people have been hunting them for centuries and there was a lot of activity in the Victorian era." Uh, no.

So, you Buffy fans. You know how Principle Snyder blamed

everything that happened at the high school on a street gang high on PCP? Here's the bookish version.

Real Victorian Slayer's Kit?

In October 2014, the *Daily Mail* in the UK reported on a vampire slaying kit that was part of a "Terror and Wonder" exhibit at the British Library in London. All of the items in the wooden box were authentic Victorian pieces, but they may have been assembled as recently as the 1930s for specialty collectors.

The museum curator speculated that about 60-70 of the kits are floating around out there. The tools included a crucifix, rosary, four stakes and a mallet, and a pistol, and vials of Holy Water.

In a post for the British Library's blog, the curator of the firearms at the United Kingdom's National Museum of Arms and Armour, offered a theory about the origin of the kit:

"Museums do collect deliberate fakes as comparators and for their own artistic and cultural merit, yet vampire kits are not fakes per se, because there is no evidence of a Victorian original. So, if they're not fake, and not reproductions, what are they? The answer is that they are 'hyperreal' or invented artifacts somewhat akin to stage, screen or magician's props."

Two years early in another *Daily Mail* story one of the kits then up for auction (and expected to fetch £2000 / $2967) was featured. These were the exact contents:

- rosary
- crucifix
- handwritten scripture
- pistol
- four stakes
- bottle of consecrated earth
- Book of Common Prayer (dated 1857)
- wooden mallet
- silver bullet mold
- cloth
- bottle of holy water
- bottle of garlic paste

The scripture, Luke 20:24 reads, "Bid those mine enemies which would not that I should reign over them bring hither, and slay them before me."

The actual purchase price? £7500 / $11,128

Sources:

Jeff Farrell, "Are These the Tools Terrified Victorians Kept to Protect Themselves from Vampires?" DailyMail.com, 2 October 2014.

Tom Gardner, "Ye Olde Vampire Slaying Kit: Victorian Oak Box Complete with Wooden Stakes," DailyMail.com, 7 June 2012.

A Modern, Practical Approach

Okay, I'm back. So, the antique kits are really cool and I wouldn't mind having one in my man cave, but carrying around a big ole box of stuff is not practical. What should you keep on your person to deal with vamps?

Like I said, I'm a talisman kind of guy, so I go with the standard silver cross because I have personal faith in it. That's the thing about any kind of religious / spiritual talisman. If you don't believe in the thing, it's just bling.

In my book on zombie survival, *Zombie Apocalypse: A Survival Guide,* I talked a lot about Altoid tin survival kits. I love me some Altoids ® tins. For $1.50 / £1.01 you get:

- length 3 13/16th inches (9.68 cm)
- width 2 7/16th inches (6.19 cm)
- depth 3/4 inch (1.91 cm)

When you're using that space for vamp gear, start with Ultimate Survival Technologies Starflash Signal Mirror for $9.59 / £6.46. It's unbreakable, measures just 2" x 3" / 5.08 cm x 7.62 cm, floats, and is 90% more reflective than glass.

If vampires hate regular mirrors, they loathe these babies, plus there's an aiming hole, so if you can angle a light source into the vamp's eyes, you have a chance to disrupt the whole mesmerism thing.

In this limited amount of space, you're not going to be able to get much of a knife, but I am seriously in love with the

CRKT RKS MK5. It retails for $20-$25 / £13.48-£16.85.

The blade is just 3.81 inches / 9.67 cm, which isn't much, but the design let's you strap the thing to any kind of long, thick pole you can get your hands on.

That means you better get some cordage in your kit as well. Believe it or not, dental floss will do the trick. Take about 10 yards and wrap it wound a Bic-type lighter. Vamps don't do well with fire, so you want to have the option of getting a flame going, too.

The dental floss is tough enough to lash your blade to something to get yourself a weapon with some reach. But here's the deal, you want to get that steel blade silver plated or it's not going to do you much good.

You should have plenty of room left for a small bag of fresh garlic cloves. Change those out regularly. You can use your knife to smash the cloves and smear them on yourself to get the maximum stink going in a crisis. Finally, find a small plastic bottle or tube that will hold some holy water.

Clearly this is an EDC (every day carry) solution with just enough stuff to give you a fighting chance in a jam. Best case scenario you've got your pepper spray pistol with you and your crossbow pistol in the trunk of your car.

Maximum Survival Philosophy

I'm a man who believes in redundant systems. The reason I like putting my basic gear in these little tins is that you can and will carry them with you. There's a little product I like called the Be Prepared Pocket Survival Tin. (Approximate price $35 / £23.59, see bestglide.com).

It's a great solution for the lazy survivalist. If you're gonna be prepared, bro, be freaking prepared. When you're dealing with vamps, you may have to go to ground until the sun comes up. It doesn't hurt to have a basic non-paranormal kit in your day bag. You can get real inventive with some of this stuff in a pinch.

The contents include:

- Weather Resistant Tin Container, Includes Rubber Seal
- Adventurer Button Compass, NATO/U.S. Military Issue
- (10) All Weather Survival Matches, NATO/U.S. Military Issue
- (1) Derma Safe Razor Knife, U.S. Military Approved
- (1) Sewing Kit w/6 Safety Pins
- (4) MP1 Water Purification Tablets, U.S. Military Issue
- (1) Rapid Rescue Survival Whistle, SOLAS Approved, NATO Issue
- (1) Mini Survival Fishing Kit
- (1) Vinyl Tape, Waterproof Kit Seal
- (1) Type 1A Utility Cord, U.S. Military Issue/Approved
- (1) Brass Snare Wire, Trapping and Equipment Repair
- (1) Compact Emergency Signal Mirror, Daytime

Emergency Signaling
- (2) Beeswax Candles
- (1) Compact Flint Fire Starter w/Striker, Adventurer Series
- (3) Fire Starter Tinder Tabs, Adventurer Series
- (1) Adventurer Fresnel Lens Fire Starter, Adventurer Series
- (6) Band Aids/Butterfly Bandages
- (1) Pocket Wire Saw
- (1) Water Bag
- (1) Survival Instructions
- (1) Pencil
- (1) Silica Gel Desiccant, Moisture Absorbent
- (2) Survival Instruction Labels

It's a good tin, and you can add and subtract stuff to suit yourself. Point is, you need to be prepared all the time for anything. Carry two tins, or switch stuff out to make this arrangement vampire friendly, but don't leave the house unarmed.

Also, I'm kinda fond of the Leatherman Micra Multitool for roughly $25 / £16.85:

- scissors
- clip-point knife
- tweezers
- nail file/cleaner
- flat Phillips screwdriver
- extra small and medium screwdriver
- bottle opener
- ruler

All in a 2.5 inch / 6.35 cm package that just weighs 2.75 ounces 77.96 grams. Just a good thing to have in your pocket. You never know.

Practice Avoidance

The point I made earlier about the way vamps infiltrating our society at all levels stands, so it's kinda silly to talk about avoidance, but I'm trying to cover all the bases here.

If you really want to stay out of the way of vampires, don't be a fang hag, don't be a willing donor, and don't hang out at vampire clubs. Yeah, I know, I sound like your Daddy, but use some damn common sense.

If you play with the vamps and get bit, don't say Uncle Rex didn't try to warn you.

Being a Believer

You know what't the worst part of being prepared for all the shades of apocalypse staring us in the face? Putting up with shit from non-believers.

Look, there's lots of stuff I didn't believe in either until I saw it, like the Loch Ness monster — but that's a cryptozoological story for another day.

When stuff keeps happening, with a predictable pattern, like, I don't know, UFOs over Area 51 — again, a conversation for another day — I start looking at the facts.

- 1800s - Groglin Range, Cumbria. Lady Cranwell was attacked in her room by a fiend with glowing eyes that left her bleeding from the neck.

  During a second attempted attack, her brothers shot the figure, a rotted corpse, which they subsequently located in an open crypt in an adjacent graveyard. The corpse had a fresh gunshot wound.

- 1918 to 1924 - Hanover, Germany. Fritz Haarmann murdered at least 24 people. He bit many of his victims through the neck and is regarded as one of the world's first recorded serial killers. He was beheaded on April 15, 1925.

- 1969 - Highgate Cemetery, London. Animals drained of blood marked with neck wounds begin to appear. A man moves into the neighborhood. He's tall, dark, and has a hypnotic stare.

- 1977 to 1978 - Richard Chase, The Vampire of Sacramento, murdered six people, disemboweling them and drinking their blood. He chose only victims whose doors were unlocked, saying, "If the door was locked that meant you weren't welcome."

- 1980 - In Marshfield, Massachusetts, James P. Riva claimed to be a 700-year-old vampire who killed his grandmother to drink her blood.

  He then stabbed her repeatedly, shot her four times, and burned her house down to cover up his crime. In some versions of his account of these events, he said his grandmother was also a vampire.

- 1996 - In Murray, Kentucky, Roderick Ferrell, leader of a Vampire Clan, traveled with some of his followers to Eustis, Florida where he murdered his girlfriend's parents to initiate the girl into his "coven." At his arrest, Ferrell claimed to be a 500-year-old vampire named Vesago.

- 2011 - St. Petersburg, Florida. A 22-year-old waitress at Hooters, Josephine Smith, attacked a 69-year-old homeless man, biting off pieces of his face, lips, and arm after telling the man, "I am a vampire. I am going to eat you."

- 2011 - A man calling himself Caius Domitius Veiovis is charged with aggravated assault in Maine for ritualistically consuming a teenaged girl's blood.

  In 2014, the same man was set to stand trial in Massachusetts for the murder of three men. Veiovis has a forked tongue, sharpened teeth, implanted horns, and a 666 tattoo on his forehead.

- 2013 - Turkey. A 23-year-old man began slicing his own body and drinking his blood. He described his compulsion to consume blood "as urgent as breathing."

  He began stabbing and biting others to increase his supply. He was diagnosed with "dissociative identity disorder."

- 2014 - A British academic. Dr. Emyr Williams of Glyndwr University, claims to have found an underground network of as many as 15,000 vampires.

  They meet regularly to consume blood and drain energy from human volunteers. Their activities, says Williams, are hidden by the groups "well-established laws."

Okay, maybe they are just dirt bags trying to get off on an insanity plea, but I'm seeing some pretty common themes here. Vampire or no vampires?

I would hope this is stating the fricking obvious, but if a dude with a forked tongue, sharpened teeth, and a 666 tattoo comes at me, he's meeting the business end of a .45 loaded with silver bullets. You don't believe me? Try it and see what happens. I'm just saying.

Chapter 7 - Vampire Terminology

Not surprisingly, there's a lot of lingo that gets thrown around vampire culture and vampire groupies. Here's a few to get you started, but trust me, there's a lot more out there.

Every vampire movie and book has its own lingo. The same is true of vampire clubs and groupies. You'll pick it up on your own fast enough.

A

animal to call - The idea that vampires have the power to summon particular animals to do their bidding. This is associated with vampire fiction, but it is not clear if the power exists or is used by real vampires.

Anne Rice - An American author who wrote a series of novels, beginning with *Interview with the Vampire* in 1976, that ultimately spanned 11 books forming *The Vampire Chronicles* that culminated in 2014 with *Prince Lestat*.

B

banking - The practice of vampires taking blood from blood banks and hospital stores.

Bela Lugosi - A Hungarian-American actor born Béla Ferenc Dezsó Blaskó. Best known for his portrayal of Count Dracula in a 1931 film.

bloodsucker - A slang term for vampires.
Bram Soker - An Irish author who wrote the classic Gothic vampire novel, *Dracula*, in 1897.

C

casket - A long, narrow, rectangular box in which a corpse is buried. The lid is hinged and can be locked. Believed to be used by vampires as a resting place during the day.

chi - A Chinese term that refers to an individual's life force.

chupacabra - An animal believed to exist in parts of Mexico and Latin America that lives by sucking blood from its victims, in particular, goats.

clinical vampirism - A psychological diagnosis explaining a person's need to take and consume blood. Also called Renfield's Syndrome.

coffin - A long narrow box, typically octagonal or hexagonal in which a corpse is buried. In this form, the lid is nailed down, not hinged and locked. Believed to be used by vampires as a resting place during the day.

D

dhampir - A vampire / human hybrid produced from the mating of a male vampire to a female human. Dhampirs have all the powers of their male parent and none of the vulnerabilities.

donor - A sarcastic name for a human who willingly opens a vein for a vampire to feed.

Dracula - The central character of the 1897 novel of the same name by Bram Stoker, now regarded as a prototypical vampire.

F

femoral artery - The large artery in the thigh that is the main supply of blood to the lower limb. A favorite alternative bite point for vampires as the wound is hidden unlike fang marks on the neck.

G

garlic - The plant most reputed to repel vampires.

H

haematomania - The strong psychological craving for blood.

hematophageous - A creature for whom blood is their only source of nutrition.

haematophilia - A sexual attraction to blood.

hematology - The clinical and scientific study of blood.

Holy Water - Water that has been blessed by a priest for use in religious ceremonies and is believed to repel vampires when wielded by someone who has faith in its powers.

The Hunger - A reference to a vampire's need to feed.

I

immortal - In its pure definition, immortal means something that cannot die. It is used freely with vampires because, if they manage to elude detection and execution, they can, in theory, live forever.

incubus - A male demon that feeds on the sexual energy of women.

K

The Kiss - Sometimes used to refer to a vampire's bite.

L

lamia - A mythical monster, half woman, half snake, who is believed by many to have been the first vampire. The scorned lover of Zeus, cursed by Hera.

Lilith - In Hebrew mythology, the first woman, created before Eve, who refused to be subservient to Adam. Believed by many sources to have become the first vampire.

Lon Chaney - An American actor best known for his portrayal of Larry Talbot, a man cursed as a werewolf in the 1941 film, *The Wolf Man*.

lycanthropy - The supernatural transformation of a human into a wolf on the full moon. Also the name given to the psychological condition of a person who believes such a transformation can or will occur.

M

Master Vampire - A term sometimes used for vampires that are extremely old and powerful.

mesmerism - A form of mind control achieved by hypnotizing a person. Vampires usually do this with their eyes and voices.

N

nest - A community of vampires that live together as a unit.

Nosferatu - A Romanian word that has come to be a synonym for "vampire." Also the title of a 1922 classic vampire film.

P

porphyria - A group of physical disorders that cause sufferers to react strongly to sunlight. Affected individuals suffer burned, blistered, and scarred skin. One of several attempted medical explanations for the symptoms of vampirism.

R

Renfield - A slang term for a vampire's human servant.

Renfield's Syndrome - A common name for clinical vampirism, which is the psychological explanation for a being's need to take and consume blood.

retainer - A human who works in the service of a vampire.

revenant - Any creature that has returned from the dead to walk among the living.

S

silver - A precious metal that, in a metaphysical sense, is believed to have protective qualities including killing werewolves and driving back vampires.

sire - A vampire's "parent." A vampire who has created another vampire.

stake - A length of wood sharpened to a point that, when driven into a vampire's heart, places the creature in a state of suspended animation until the stake is removed.

succubus - A female demon that feeds on the sexual energy of men.

supernatural - Anything that is attributed to a force beyond the known realm of science.

V

vampirology - Regarded as a sub-discipline of demonology for academic purposes, this is the organized study of vampires.

Van Helsing - A character in Bram Stoker's novel *Dracula*, and a slang term for a vampire hunter.

W

werewolf - A person who, on the full moon, transforms into a wolf as a consequence of having been cursed or because they are suffering from lycanthropy.

X

xenophobia - The fear and hatred of things foreign.

Z

zombies - The reanimated dead that, unlike vampires, do not retain their intellectual capacity and are driven by mindless hunger alone.

Afterword

I'm gonna leave you with kind of an egghead thought on this subject. Bram Stoker wrote *Dracula* in 1897, but the guy who made the Transylvanian count a pop culture standard was Bela Lugosi. Poor schmuck really was cursed by the vampire.

Lugosi was a classically trained Shakespearean actor with a Hungarian accent so thick you couldn't cut it with a knife. In 1927, he did a Broadway version of *Dracula* and sealed his own fate. He never escaped being Dracula and even today when most people think Dracula, it's Bela Lugosi they have in mind.

Part of the reason the play, and then the 1931 movie version were so big is that Americans were out of their gourds scared of foreigners back then. They had a major case of xenophobia tinged with anti-Communism and here was a foreign-sounding dude playing the most alien thing imaginable, a vampire. The whole picture screamed threat and was extra scary because of it.

But here's the really scary part to me. Actual vampires know how to study the press they're getting. Being portrayed as outsiders is not good for achieving their modern, long-term goal — legal social status and political power.

So along comes Anne Rice forty years later and she's suddenly writing about these conflicted, sensitive, worldly vampires who sit around sipping blood out of fine crystal and talking all this existential crap about who they are and why they're here.

You know the story about the frog and the scorpion? Scorpion needs to get across a flooded river and tries to get the frog to carry him over. Frog says, "No way, you'll bite me." Scorpion says, "Why would I do that? We'd both just die." So the frog gives in.

Half-way across the river, the scorpion stings him. As they're going down, the frog says, "Why did you do that? You've just killed yourself, too." The scorpion says, "Because that's just the kind of S.O.B. I am."

Existential debate my big fat backside. Vampires do what they do because that's just the kind of S.O.B.s they are. They're not driven by angst, they're driven by a strong instinct to survive and the ambition to survive *well*.

From Anne Rice forward, vampires in the popular perception have turned into just another class of troubled souls in need of a shot of empathy and O-positive. Loser groupies have made bloodsucking the new alternative lifestyle.

That, my friends, is indeed a set up for an apocalypse. But again, not the messy kind like the world going south if the zombie thing breaks first. This "apocalypse" is actually gonna be more like the most elegant political coup you've ever seen.

You do what you like. Go ahead and ignore the threat. Buy

the bleeding heart vampire civil rights crap. Believe they're just like us. And do not come crying to me when it's game over, people. You and Renfield, in the nut house, eating bugs. Have fun with that.

Relevant Websites

"9 People Who Are Definitely Real Life Vampires"
www.ifc.com/fix/2014/07/9-people-who-are-definitely-real-
life-vampires

"The 10 Best Vampire Novels No One Has Read"
www.barnesandnoble.com/blog/the-10-best-vampire-
novels-no-one-has-read/

"10 Creepy Historical Vampires You've Never Heard Of"
listverse.com/2013/08/11/10-vampires-from-history-youve-
never-heard-of/

"The 20 Best Modern Vampire Moves, 1979 to the Present"
blogs.villagevoice.com/runninscared/2014/10/the_best_vam
pire_movies_1979_to_the_present.php

"The Best Ways to Defeat a Vampire"
www.dummies.com/how-to/content/the-best-ways-to-
defeat-a-vampire.html

"Do Vampires Prefer a Certain Type of Human Blood?"
mysticinvestigations.com/paranormal/do-vampires-prefer-
a-certain-type-of-blood/

"The Emotional Vampire Survival Guide: Emotional
Freedom in Action"
www.drjudithorloff.com/Free-Articles/Emotional-Vampire-
survival.htm

"The Medical Truth Behind the Vampire Myths"
amarisgrey.wordpress.com/2008/07/29/the-medical-truth-
behind-the-vampire-myths/

"Meet the Real-Life Vampires of New England and
Abroad"
www.smithsonianmag.com/history/meet-the-real-life-
vampires-of-new-england-and-abroad-42639093/?no-ist

"Nature Against Vampires"
www.vampires.com/nature-against-vampires

"Real-Live 'Vampire' Addicted to Blood, Doctors Claim"
www.livescience.com/26971-real-life-vampire-addicted-to-
blood.html

"Top 10 Most Awesome Vampire Movies Ever Made"
moviepilot.com/posts/2013/11/04/top-10-most-awesome-
vampire-movies-ever-made-
1164666?lt_source=external,manual,manual

"The Top 10 Vampire Books"
www.theguardian.com/books/2014/oct/29/top-10-vampire-
books

"Famous Vampire Victims"
www.fvza.org/vvictims.html

"Vampires and Blood Types"
thevampireproject.blogspot.com/2009/01/vampires-and-
blood-types.html

"Vampires: Fact, Fiction and Folklore"
www.livescience.com/24374-vampires-real-history.html

"The Vampire Myth and Christianity"
scholarship.rollins.edu/mls/16/

"Vampire Pathology"
www.vampyreverse.com/facts/pathology.shtml

"Ways to Identify a Potential Vampire"
www.vampires.com/ways-to-identify-a-potential-vampire

"Why Can't Vampires Enter a Home Without Being
Invited?"
mysticinvestigations.com/paranormal/why-cant-vampires-
enter-a-home-without-being-invited/

Index

Feeding Baby
Cynthia Cherry
978-1941070000

Axolotl
Lolly Brown
978-0989658430

Dysautonomia, POTS
Syndrome
Frederick Earlstein
978-0989658485

Degenerative Disc
Disease Explained
Frederick Earlstein
978-0989658485

Sinusitis, Hay Fever,
Allergic Rhinitis Explained
Frederick Earlstein
978-1941070024

Wicca
Riley Star
978-1941070130

Zombie Apocalypse
Rex Cutty
978-1941070154

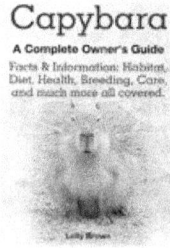

Capybara
Lolly Brown
978-1941070062

Eels As Pets
Lolly Brown
978-1941070167

Scabies and Lice Explained
Frederick Earlstein
978-1941070017

Saltwater Fish As Pets
Lolly Brown
978-0989658461

Torticollis Explained
Frederick Earlstein
978-1941070055

Kennel Cough
Lolly Brown
978-0989658409

Physiotherapist, Physical
Therapist
Christopher Wright
978-0989658492

Rats, Mice, and Dormice
As Pets
Lolly Brown
978-1941070079

Wallaby and Wallaroo Care
Lolly Brown
978-1941070031

Bodybuilding Supplements
Explained
Jon Shelton
978-1941070239

Demonology
Riley Star
978-19401070314

Pigeon Racing
Lolly Brown
978-1941070307